In for Winter, Out for Spring

In for Winter, Out for Spring

By ARNOLD ADOFF

Illustrations by JERRY PINKNEY

Harcourt Brace Jovanovich, Publishers

SAN DIEGO   NEW YORK   LONDON

HBJ

Text copyright © 1991 by Arnold Adoff
Illustrations copyright © 1991 by Jerry Pinkney

Library of Congress Cataloging-in-Publication Data
Adoff, Arnold.
In for winter, out for spring/by Arnold Adoff;
illustrations by Jerry Pinkney. — 1st ed.
p.   cm.
Summary: This collection of poems, told from the
perspective of a young girl, celebrates family life
throughout the yearly cycle of seasons.
ISBN 0-15-238637-8
1. Seasons — Juvenile poetry. 2. Children's poetry, American.
[1. Seasons — Poetry. 2. Family life — Poetry. 3. American poetry.]
I. Pinkney, Jerry, ill. II. Title.
PS3551.D66I6   1991
811'.54 — dc20   90-33185

First edition
A B C D E

The illustrations in this book were done in pencil, watercolor,
color pencil, and pastel on 130-lb. Arches hot-press paper.

The text type was set in Berling by Thompson Type, San Diego, California.

The display type was set in Pictor Medium by Central Graphics, San Diego, California.

Color separations were made by Bright Arts, Ltd., Singapore.

Printed and bound by Tien Wah Press, Singapore

Production supervision by Warren Wallerstein and Ginger Boyer

Typography by Michael Farmer

For my mother and father: Rebecca Stein Adoff and Aaron Jacob Adoff
—A. A.

In celebration of the family
—J. P.

I Am The Youngest   So They Call
                    Me   All
                    Day Long

My Name Is Rebecca At Breakfast
                         Time
          Becky By Lunch
                         But
     Becka
     Beck
     Beck Come
          Wash   Your
                    Neck
     Is Daddy's Supper
          Song

                    I Like My Real
                    Name   Short
                    And   My Hair
                    Real   Long
I Am The Youngest   And I Belong

This House   Is The   Center

Is My   Home
Is Where
    My   Toys
            Belong
Is Where
    My   Brother
            Aaron
            Sleeps

This House
Has   Food
Has   Mom
        And
        Dad
Has   My
       Great
       Bed   This   Winter
                      Season
                      Under
                      Snow

We   Know
This House   Is The   Center

The First Flakes   Are Falling   On Our Heads

As Daddy Stands Me Up Against The Cold Back
                                          Door
For My Morning Measurement
                          Of Course This
                                 Head
                                 Line
              Is   Higher Than The Last
                                 Head
                                 Line
But This Will Be The Last Time   Until   The
                               Snows
Are Over   And We Can Get Outside Again   For
                        Morning Chores

Now I Know That Daddy And Aaron   Will   Bake
Their Best Cookies   And Momma Will Make
The Most Crisp   Chicken   That Helps To Grow
                            Us   All
In This Long Winter House Under Snow

In The Ending   Of This Evening Snow

I Like My Long Hair Free   Let It Blow
                         Let It Blow

In The   Last   Light
Of The   Last   S u n
            Glow   Let It Blow
                         Let It Blow

I Am Some Wild Horse
Running From   Fence
                 To
           Fence
My Hot Breath
        Blowing
In The Wild
        Evening
         Freeze
          And I Am Free As My L o n g
                        Hair   Blows
           Like That Horse Mane In The
                        Snow Breeze
                        Let It Blow
                        Let It Blow

In The Ending   Of This Evening Snow
I Like My Long Hair Free

Mouse   Under The House   Mouse   In The House

One Day   In This Coldest Winter   But In Our
                                            W a r m
                                            Kitchen
Daddy   Screamed   A Perfect
Cartoon Scream   And Dropped   The Heavy Cream
                   And Dropped   His C a k e   Pan
                                        A n d Ran
                            Out   Of   Our
                                        W a r m
                                        Kitchen
                Faster   Than   The   Mouse Was
                R u n n i n g   The   Other Way

Later On   We Explored Outside   And Found A Crack In The
    Foundation Stones Big Enough For A Whole Family Of Cold
And Hungry Mice   And All Their Luggage   They Must Have
Traveled Through The Heating Ducts That Lie   Under The
    House From Room To Room Until They Settled In The Warm
    Kitchen In Back Of The Cabinet Next To The W a r m Oven
Their
Nest Was Between Two Bags Of Daddy's   Best   Cake   Flour
And An Old Pot   Full   Of   Soft   White   String   I Think
                They Were Planning To Stay Until Spring

Out For Spring

I
Sing And   Shout
             About
             Time
     For
     Big
     Bad Winter
          Times
            To
           End
I
Send
This   Spring
          Song
           Out
     For
     All
     To   Shout
     And Sing

Out For Spring
Out For Spring
Out For Spring

After The Last Hard Freeze   In Early Spring Weather

When The Ground Has Softened   And The Sun Is Strong
Enough To Warm The Open Field   We Dig Up The   Young
                                                      Sumac
                                                      Saplings

From Their   Winter Places   Beside The Old
                                              Fence
And Carry Them To   New
                      Places In   Our   Front
                                              Yard

I Am Digging Holes With Daddy   Spreading Roots   Out
I Am Filling   Holes With Rich Dirt And Peat
                                              Moss   Pouring
                                                         In
                                Green Fertilizer Water
                                For A Healthy Start
                                In Their New Homes

I Am Digging Holes With Daddy

She   Was   Hungry   And   Cold

Alone
Along The Edge   Of Granny's Field
A   Tired   Puppy   Chased
By   Fresh   Farm   Dogs   And   Their
                  P l o w i n g   Farmer
                              To My
                              Yard

I   Am   Building   Her   New   House
And   Will   Take   Care   Of Her From
                          N o w On
            And Momma Says She Can
                              Stay

                              Stray

I Hear The Usual   Thump

And Know That One   More
                           R o b i n
Has Hit The Glass   Door
In Love   With   Its   Own
                           Reflection

This Bird Seems To
                       Be
R e s t i n g
       On The
       Ground
T e s t i n g   Its Bent
                      W i n g

I   Bring
A   Dish
Of Water And   Watch   For
                  C a t s

On   May   Day

        This
     Monarch
     Butterfly
Flew
Into   Our
Open Door
       And
Through
        The
House   To
Land   On
        Top
        Of
        My
Open
Hand

        Of
     Course
I   Set
It   Free

The Morning Wind   From The West

Is Bringing The Smoke
Of The Paper Mills
         And
         The
              Smoke
Of Burning
    Plastic And Coal

Some Days   The   Air   Is So Good
It Is The Best Cure For Bad Dreams
But This Morning
    This Air   Is
              Bad
              For All Living Things
              The
              Breeze   Brings   Ills
              The Wind   Seems   Sad
              To Be Blowing Our Way

We Stay In For The Rest Of The Day

My Brother Aaron Runs Outside To Tell Us There Is A Severe
                                        Thunder
                                        Storm
                                        Warning

Just Announced On The Radio While We Were Out
                                    U n d e r
A Perfectly Blue Sky
We Know How Fast The   Weather Can Change   How
                          Fast Those   Storms   Can
                          Blow Across These   Corn
                          Fields   E v e r y   Spring

We Bring   Our   Books
And Toys Inside   And
Listen To   The   Noon
                   News
Between   The Soup
And   Sandwiches
And
Try To Only Think
              A b o u t
              Our Lunch

Clouds Are Black

      And
      Dark Green   This Afternoon
And They
Are Sitting   Over Our Town
           Just Rumb l i n g
               A w a y
With Their Bragging
      N o i s e

Who Ordered
The Thunder
Who Ordered That Flash Of Lightning
           Flashing From The
                    West
Who Ordered The Rest Of   This Dark Sky

Who Asked This S t o r m To S t a y

The Bottoms   Of My Sneaks   Are   Green

Then
The Bottoms   Of My Sweat   Are   Green
                        Socks
Then
The Bottoms   Of My F e e t   Turn   Green
                                    As
When
        My Sneaks And   Socks   Come   Off
                                Half   Way
                                Down
                                This
                                Field   Of
                                Fresh
                                        Green
                                        Grass
                                And
                                Dew

My Momma Mows
This   N e w
            Summer
            Morning

Daddy   Is Tall   Has Shoulders   Strong Hands

But I Am   The   Mulberry   Girl
Riding   On His High Shoulders   Under These
Tree
Treats
These
H a n g i n g
B r a n c h e s
These
H a n g i n g
Eats

So   Dry   This   July

          This
                    Drought
Has   Cracked
The   Ground
Has   Killed
          Young
          Trees

When It   Finally   Does
                    Rain
Good   And   Hard
We Run   Into   The   Yard
To   Soak   Our
Dusty   Feet   In   Mud
          Up   To
                    Our
                    Knees

Volunteers   One

Black Raspberry Bushes   Blackberries
Wild Strawberries   Wild Onion Grass
Dandelions   Mint   Catnip   Maples
                    F o r S h a d e
Elm And Ash   And Sunflowers   Daisies
Wild Roses   Poison Ivy So Thick You
                    Know To Stay Far Away
Black Walnut
        Trees

                For
                Our Cakes   And Hungry
                        S q u i r r e l s
                Who Will
                        Stay   For The Wet
                        W i n t e r
And
All The Trees   And Weeds   And   Wild
                                F l o w e r s

And Their Blowing   Seeds

Volunteers   Two

Clouds Of Flies When The Hot Dogs Are Done
                    And We Are Ready To Eat
Mosquitoes And Bugs That Fly In Your Ears
                    And Gnats
                    And Mayflies
                    And Devilflies That Bite   In
                                                    The
                                                    Heat
                              Of   A Dry   July
                                                    After
                                                    noon

Bees All Do Their Famous Work
         And Worms Are Washed   Up
                              After
                              Rains
         And Spiders
         Spiders
         Spiders

One Night

They   Are
         Out
         All
Together
On
Some
Signal   At
The
Same Time
F l a s h i n g
      And
F l a s h i n g
      And
B l i n k i n g
Bright   in
      This
      Late
   Summer
     Night
Long
Past   My
Bed   Time
Late   This
     Night
Of
The
F i r e f l i e s

I Know That Summer Is The Famous Growing Season

But These Fall Days Are For The Gathering Of
                                             The
                                             Last
                                             Of
                                             The
Grown And Ripe Tomatoes
For G r a n n y ' s Tomato
                Preserves   Corn and Beans   To Be
                Canned   In Mason Jars

I Get To Climb The Old Apple Tree   For The Best
                Yellow   Delicious Apples
For Daddy's Pie
For Momma's Apple Honey Buns
For My C l i m b i n g F u n

Daddy Carries His Empty Basket

On His Head
And Pretends To Be A Boy Worker
On
This Farm
I Carry My Basket
Under   My   Arm
And Pretend To Be
The   Grown
Owner Of The   Entire   Territory
To The Far Hills Beyond

We   Pretend A Farmer Planted This   Tree
A Hundred Years Ago To Keep
The Strong West Winds   From
Hitting
His House So Hard
Or   Maybe
Those

Winds   Carried Some Tree S e e d s
Over The Hill To Our Yard
We   Will
Never Know But Those Black
Walnuts Make The Best Cake

Sunday Afternoon   Under A Warm Blue Sky

We Stop Our Game   To Notice A Busy Chip
                                    munk
Digging New Tunnels   At The Edge
                          Of Our Yard

Our Family Squirrel   Stops
                    In   Front   Of   His
                                T r e e
With A Fresh Black Walnut   In His Mouth
We
See Him Go Up And Down That Tree   A l l
                        A f t e r n o o n
With Supplies For Long
                Cold   M o n t h s

As A Cloud
Passes Over The Warm Sun   We Feel   That
                                    First
                                    Cool
                                    Hint

Aaron

My Older Brother
Once Told Me He
Was The Ruler Of   This Hedge
Last
Year I Had To Have Permission
To Pick Wild Violets   For Mom

This   Morning   Aaron
                                    Sits
                                    In A
                                    School
And I Am   The New Boss
Of Hedge Trees
And Mole Holes
And Violets   And   Black Bugs
                                    Under
                                    Green
                                    Moss

Before The End   Of This Falling Fall Day

When Night
        Means
                End Of Play
                And
                Put The Toys
                        A w a y
There Is Almost
                Dark   When The Field Is Full
                        Of S e c r e t s Under
                        The   H e a v y Hedge

Cicadas   Sound   Electric
Catbirds Sound Like Cats
Even Jays Are Fooled In
                        to
W a r n i n g   S q u a w k s

                                    Hawks
                                C i r c l e
                                    Their
                                Baby Hawks
                                    Home

Granny's Ninety-Two-Year-Old Legs

Are Aching This October Morning   The Sun Is Bright   In The Pale
                                                                   Blue
                                                                   Sky
But She Says Her Shin Bones Have Been Hurting   Clear To   Winter

There Will Be   Falling
           Weather By The Feel Of Her Legs   And   She Knows
                   That   Barometer   At The Weather Station
                   Will   Follow   Right   Along   By   Evening
                   And There Will Be Cold And Rain Through
                                        The   Night

Granny's Ninety-Two-Year-Old   Legs
                                   Are
                                 Almost
                                 Always
                                 Right

October
Afternoons   We Walk Around The House

Pulling Chair Cushions Into The Garage
And Covering The Round White Table Where
We Ate Last S u m m e r ' s Snacks
And Stacking All The Chairs And Tables
U n t i l N e x t S p r i n g
I Bring
  Daddy
  Some
    Nails While He Hammers Bent Boards In
                                      to
        T h e O l d Y a r d F e n c e

Saturday   After Aaron's Soccer Game   He
                                        Gets
                                          To
        Walk The Dog Around Our   House
        While We Put   New Straw   Into
                                      The
                                      Dog
                                    House
        And A Nice Piece Of Purple Rug
        F o r T h e C o l d F l o o r

It   Is   Late

When We Walk   Back From Our Healthy Walk Tonight
The
Moon Is So Full   It Is Almost   Bursting   O   p   e   n
                    Like That Over
                         ripe Pumpkin In   Our
                                          G a r d e n
The
Moon Is Hanging Like That   Pumpkin A   F   a   c   e
                                  Without
                                               Over
                                               Our
                                          H e d g e

We Want To   Carve   A Face
Into
This Harvest Moon Tonight And Have It Grin An
                             Autumn   Greeting
                             In   The   Fall Air

                             Seeds Of   Starlight
                             S c a t t e r   Everywhere

On   Limestone   Street

Where The   Open Field Is Longest   Back   To
The   Minnow   Stream WePutOurBikesDown
                                        And   L i s t e n
This Must Be The N o i s i e s t Day   Of   This
                                        End   Of   This
                                        Fall S e a s o n

Woodpeckers   Peck Wood
And Bluejays   Screech
And Each   Cold B r e e z e
           Hard
Blows Branches   Shakes
                        Leaves
Over Our Freezing Ears

Near Our Fence
Farmer Frances Is Cutting Dead Trees For Her
                            W a r m i n g
                                Fires

We Will All Be
In For Winter
Very   Soon